To my beloved "Señorita Swing"
(a.k.a. Carol Morrissey Greiner)
—T. deP.

For Michael Frith,
artist, mentor, friend
—J. L.

SIMON & SCHUSTER BOOKS FOR YOUNG READERS
An imprint of Simon & Schuster Children's Publishing Division
1230 Avenue of the Americas, New York, New York 10020
Text copyright © 2017 by Tomie dePaola and Jim Lewis
Illustrations copyright © 2017 by Tomie dePaola
SIMON & SCHUSTER BOOKS FOR YOUNG READERS
is a trademark of Simon & Schuster, Inc.
For information about special discounts for bulk purchases, please contact Simon & Schuster
Special Sales at 1-866-506-1949 or business@simonandschuster.com.
The Simon & Schuster Speakers Bureau can bring authors to your live event.
For more information or to book an event, contact the Simon & Schuster Speakers Bureau
at 1-866-248-3049 or visit our website at www.simonspeakers.com.
Book design by Laurent Linn
The text for this book was set in Minister Std.
The illustrations for this book were rendered in acrylics with colored pencil
on 150lb Fabriano Cold Press 100% rag watercolor paper.
Manufactured in China
0119 SCP
First Simon & Schuster Books for Young Readers paperback edition April 2019
2 4 6 8 10 9 7 5 3 1
The Library of Congress has cataloged the hardcover edition as follows:
Names: DePaola, Tomie, 1934- author, illustrator. | Lewis, Jim, 1955- author.
Title: Andy & Sandy and the big talent show / Tomie dePaola ; cowritten with Jim Lewis.
Other titles: Andy and Sandy and the big talent show
Description: First edition. | New York : Simon & Schuster Books for Young Readers, [2017] |
Series: An Andy & Sandy book | Summary: "Andy and Sandy are entering the big talent show!
Sandy can juggle. Sandy can tumble. Sandy can hula hoop. Andy cannot do any of these things.
But when Sandy is the one who gets stage fright, Andy can save the day!"—Provided by publisher.
Identifiers: LCCN 2016036056 | ISBN 9781481479479 (hardcover) |
ISBN 9781534413757 (pbk) | ISBN 9781481479486 (eBook)
Subjects: | CYAC: Talent shows—Fiction. | Ability—Fiction. | Stage fright—Fiction. |
Best friends—Fiction. | Friendship—Fiction.
Classification: LCC PZ7.D439 Ad 2017 | DDC [E]—dc23
LC record available at https://lccn.loc.gov/2016036056

Andy & Sandy
and the
Big Talent Show

Tomie dePaola
COWRITTEN WITH Jim Lewis

SIMON & SCHUSTER BOOKS FOR YOUNG READERS
New York London Toronto Sydney New Delhi

We should enter!

What's my talent?

Can you
juggle?

Can you
tumble?

Can you hula hoop?

I cannot do that

or that

or that.

We can do a dance—
together!

I cannot do that, either!

It is easy.
Follow me.

You just have to practice.

Psst, Sandy.
Follow me.

The winners!

Now we take a bow—

together.

ANDY'S BACKSTAGE
THE COSTUME SHOP

TIGHTS

COSTUMES ON THE RACK

HATS

SHOES

ANDY